T0132249

Cowboy Flash

Charlie Alexander

Cowboy Flash

Written by Charles Alexander
Artwork by Charlie Alexander

Yippee!

Flash was pretty good at lassoing.

Flash was in charge of driving the covered wagon.

He just needed a couple horses to pull.

Flash went to find his clothes.

He couldn't wait to try on his new boots!

Everybody thought Flash's boots were the top!!

Flash thought he was really cool.

It was time to show off.

Flash's new cowboy shirt was really fancy.

Flash loved his new cowboy hat!

It fit perfectly and stayed on even on a windy day.

The barn stored all the hay!

It was big and very red.

Flash had painted a second coat of paint.

He sure did a good job!

All the cowboys were thirsty.

They enjoyed the cold water from the canteen!

It was time for a new saddle.

Flash had lots of riding to do!

He still liked his red saddle a lot.

He was fond of his hat as well.

The stagecoach was so much fun to drive

Flash had to wait for the horses to be harnessed.

Flash was ready to try his new saddlebag.

He was preparing two horses for a cattle drive.

The horses were saddled.

Flash was excited about his new brown saddle!

Flash rode his pony Roland in the cattle drive.

The cows mood very loudly.

The cows didn't know where to go.

They needed Flash's direction.

Flash loved making a fire.

It was time to start making lunch.

Pizza and hamburgers are being served.

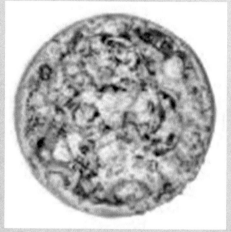

A nice drink of lemonade cured a mighty thirst.

The Indian chief was dressed in his
feathers and suit.

Flash was happy that the chief was coming to lunch.

After lunch came desert.

Watermelon and ice cream hit the spot.

Don't forget the water bucket Flash.

He went to the well and filled the bucket full of water.

Of course Flash made sure the fire was extinguished.

He poured water on it to be sure it was out!

The sheriff was too late for lunch.

He was waiting for his wife to join him.

She wore a green skirt and matching hat.

Everyone was happy to see Angela.

After desert, the sheriff and his wife had to leave.

His office was in the middle of town.

There were lots of cacti along the way.

Flash quickly learned they were sharp and pointy.

Flash had to go help brand some of the cattle.

No problem. Flash was on the job.

Flash knew how to brand them.

It was his least favorite task.

A buffalo said " Please don't brand me".

"I'm a buffalo and don't need to be branded".

It was a full day of hard work.

A ride in a canoe was great before getting ready for church.

It was a beautiful evening to go to church.

The service began at 7 pm sharp!

Flash looked up!

He thought he saw ice cream cones in the sky!

It was a pleasure to see the stars after a busy day.

It was dark enough to see that the sky was full of stars.

This beautiful gift was for Flash.

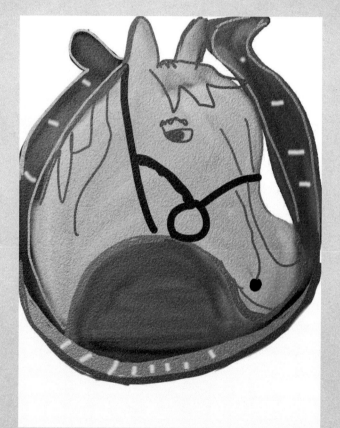

Every one was proud of him!
The End

To order additional copies of this book, contact:
Xlibris
844-714-8691
www.Xlibris.com
Orders@Xlibris.com

ISBN: Softcover   978-1-6698-7689-2
          Hardcover   978-1-6698-7688-5
          EBook   978-1-6698-7690-8

Library of Congress Control Number: 2023908701

Print information available on the last page

Rev. date: 05/09/2023

Printed in the United States
by Baker & Taylor Publisher Services